The Forbidden Island: A Race Against Time

Eliza Grey

Published by RWG Publishing, 2023.

This is a work of fiction. Similarities to real people, places, or events are entirely coincidental.

THE FORBIDDEN ISLAND: A RACE AGAINST TIME

First edition. May 16, 2023.

Copyright © 2023 Eliza Grey.

Written by Eliza Grey.

Also by Eliza Grey

The School for Gifted Teens: A Young Adult Fantasy
The Secret Society of the Night: A Young Adult Mystery
The Forbidden Island: A Race Against Time

Table of Contents

Chapter 1: The Discovery of the Forbidden Island 1
Chapter 2: The Legend of the Island's Curse 5
Chapter 3: A Desperate Journey Begins 9
Chapter 4: A Race Against Time 13
Chapter 5: The Island's Many Secrets 17
Chapter 6: The Arrival of the First Obstacle 19
Chapter 7: The Search for Clues 21
Chapter 8: An Unexpected Ally 23
Chapter 9: The First Showdown 25
Chapter 10: Escaping the Danger 27
Chapter 11: The Island's Mysterious Wildlife 29
Chapter 12: Into the Heart of Darkness 31
Chapter 13: The Second Obstacle Appears 33
Chapter 14: Uncovering the Island's Dark History 35
Chapter 15: A Deadly Trap 37
Chapter 16: Fighting for Survival 41
Chapter 17: A Glimmer of Hope 45
Chapter 18: The Third Obstacle Looms 47
Chapter 19: The Final Battle Approaches 49
Chapter 20: The Island's Greatest Secret 51
Chapter 21: Racing Against the Clock 53
Chapter 22: The Tides Turn 55
Chapter 23: The End is Near 57
Chapter 24: A Heroic Sacrifice 59
Chapter 25: A Narrow Escape 61
Chapter 26: The Aftermath 63
Chapter 27: A New Dawn 65
Chapter 28: The Journey Home 67
Chapter 29: A Bittersweet Victory 69
Chapter 30: Return to the Forbidden Island 71

Chapter 1: The Discovery of the Forbidden Island

Captain James McCallister stood at the railing and observed the vastness of the blue ocean before him. He had been at sea for months, during which time his crew had become worn out and antsy. The monotony was broken when the lookout, who was stationed in the crow's nest high above, yelled down to his fellow soldiers that he had spotted something on the horizon.

McCallister made a beeline for the deck as he scanned the horizon with his eyes. At first, all he could see was the sea and the sky, but then he suddenly caught a glimpse of something off in the distance. It was an island that was completely different from any other that he had ever seen before. The island was covered in fog, and the jagged peaks of the surrounding mountains poked out of the clouds in unexpected places. It was an ominous scene, and McCallister knew at once that he needed to investigate it even though he was scared.

After receiving the order to alter course, the captain turned the ship in the direction of the island. As they got closer, McCallister was able to make out that the island was very rocky and covered in dense vegetation. It also had precipitous cliffs that dropped off into the water. Although it was a dangerous environment, McCallister was adamant that he would investigate it.

As they got closer to the island, the crew noticed that a feeling of unease was beginning to take hold of them. There was a palpable sense of tension in the air, and the island itself seemed to give off a peculiar kind of energy. However, McCallister was unfazed and gave the order for the ship to anchor itself in the water just offshore.

Following the lowering of a small boat into the water by the crew, McCallister and a select few of his most reliable men boarded the vessel. They proceeded to row in the direction of the island, the sound of their oars reverberating off the surrounding cliffs.

They were beginning to get closer when they noticed that the island was even more formidable when viewed up close. They were dwarfed by the cliffs, which were accompanied by the deafening roar of the waves as they crashed against the rocks. As they made their way closer to the shore, the forest was gloomy and ominous, and it gave the impression that it was going to consume them.

At last, they arrived at a secluded bay, and there, McCallister gave the order for the men to row ashore. They were walking on sand that was dark and gritty, and the air was heavy with the smell of salt and seaweed.

McCallister was in charge of leading the way, and his eyes were constantly on the lookout for any indication of impending danger. They maneuvered their way through the thick forest using a winding path that was only a few feet wide. The branches of the trees constantly brushed against their faces and arms. The echo of their footsteps could be heard throughout the forest, and the stillness around them seemed to be closing in on them.

After what seemed like an eternity, they came out into the open. An odd assortment of carvings and symbols were etched into the stone of the altar, which stood in the middle of the open space. McCallister approached it with extreme caution while his heart was thumping wildly in his chest.

As he approached the altar, he became aware of a peculiar energy that seemed to be emanating from it. He reached out to touch it, and the instant his fingers made contact with it, he felt a jolt of electricity shoot through his body. He quickly withdrew his hand. He winced in discomfort, but just as he was doing so, he caught a glimpse of something out of the corner of his eye.

There, on the very outskirts of the open space, one could find a sacred building. It was made of stone and covered in moss and vines, and it was an old structure. McCallister could feel the weight of history and mystery bearing down on him as he approached the entrance, which was guarded by a pair of stone statues.

He was aware that he had stumbled upon something truly remarkable, something that had the potential to alter the path of his life as well as the lives of those who were close to him. He faced his soldiers with a fierce determination in his eyes as he turned to face them.

"We have discovered something that is truly remarkable here," he stated. "We have no choice but to investigate this island in order to learn its mysteries."

The voyage of discovery had thus gotten under way.

McCallister and his crew spent weeks mapping the island's terrain and uncovering its secrets as part of their exploration of the island. They uncovered previously unknown caverns and ancient ruins, and as they proceeded further into the island, they began to come across strange animals and challenges. They had to battle their way through dangerous terrain and avoid being attacked by vicious beasts in order to succeed.

McCallister and his crew were overcome with a sense of excitement and wonder despite the perilous circumstances they were in. They were unearthing a world that had been concealed for centuries, and they were resolved to discover its long-guarded secrets.

They continued to make their way deeper into the island, and as they did so, they encountered a series of puzzles and challenges that put their resourcefulness and inventiveness to the test. They were required to solve puzzles and decode ancient texts, all while protecting themselves from the island's hostile flora and fauna.

They had been searching for what felt like weeks before they found a chamber buried deep within the temple. The room was crammed with priceless relics and antiquities from bygone eras, and McCallister immediately realized that he had stumbled upon something truly remarkable.

However, just as he and his crew were about to claim their prize, a low rumbling sound interrupted them. They became aware that an eruption was about to take place on the island when the ground started to shake beneath their feet.

They made a mad dash to get back to their ship, but the island was already in complete disarray when they arrived. The ground beneath their feet was breaking up and cracking open, and lava was pouring down from the summits of the mountains.

McCallister insisted on staying behind in order to retrieve the treasure despite the risks. As quickly as they could, he and his men made their way back to the room and grabbed as much treasure as they could carry.

The crew could feel the heat of the lava on their backs as they fled the island as quickly as they could. They rowed with all of their strength, intent on putting as much distance as possible between themselves and the island as quickly as they could.

In the end, they were able to make it back to their ship, despite the fact that their hearts were racing and their bodies were exhausted. They had made it off the island alive, but they were well aware that they had stumbled upon something astonishingly unique.

McCallister realized as they were sailing away from the island that he would one day have to go back to visit it. He had only just begun to explore its mysteries, but he was determined to find out everything it had to offer.

But for the time being, they embarked on the journey back to their homeland, eager to tell the rest of the world about their incredible discovery.

Chapter 2: The Legend of the Island's Curse

Uncertainty was palpable in the air as Captain James McCallister and his crew made their way away from the Forbidden Island in their ship. They had only just begun to scratch the surface of the island's secrets, despite the fact that the island had been shrouded in danger and mystery.

But as they continued their journey, McCallister started to overhear rumors of a myth that was associated with the island. The tale told of a curse that had been placed on the island many years ago, a curse that had befallen anyone who had the audacity to step foot on its shores. The curse was said to have killed anyone who did so.

The island was said to have been cursed by a long-forgotten people group that had once made it their home and placed a hex on it, according to the legend. The tribe had been successful and powerful in the past, but as time went on, they became haughty and self-centered.

A powerful artifact, a gemstone that was said to hold the power of the gods, had been found by the chief of the tribe one day. The chief had developed an unhealthy preoccupation with the gemstone, and as a result, he began hoarding it and refusing to give any of it to anyone else.

The members of the tribe had become agitated and enraged, and they demanded that the chief divide the gemstone between them all. However, the chief had rejected their offer, and in his pride, he dared to challenge the gods themselves.

The angered gods had retaliated by bringing a terrible curse down upon the people of the tribe and the entire island. It was said that the curse would bring a terrible end to the lives of anyone who dared to step foot on the island.

McCallister had a healthy amount of skepticism regarding the myth, but he couldn't shake the nagging feeling that there was some basis in reality to it. He made the decision to look into the rumor and see if there was any truth to the story.

After scouring ancient texts and consulting with experts in history and academia, he did eventually come across some evidence that lends credence to the myth. He made the startling discovery that the island was once home to a long-vanished civilization that was afflicted by a divine wrath brought down upon them by the gods.

It was said that the curse would cause the island to be covered in mist and darkness, and that anyone who set foot on the island's shores would be doomed to suffer a terrible fate if they did so. Over the years, many people had attempted to explore the island, but none of them had ever made it back.

McCallister was unable to withstand the allure of the Forbidden Island despite the risks involved. He was well aware that there were mysteries to be solved, and he was resolute in his pursuit of those answers.

However, as he set sail in the direction of the island, he couldn't help but feel apprehensive about what was to come. He was aware that he and his crew were playing with fate and that there was a possibility that the curse would come true.

As the crew got closer to the island, they could see that the tale was not just a made-up tall tale at all. In point of fact, the island was enveloped in mist and darkness, and the air was dense with a spooky stillness.

Following McCallister's instruction to approach the shore in a cautious manner, the crew made their way to the water's edge. As soon as they set foot on the dark sand, they were overcome with a feeling of dread that would not leave them alone.

They started exploring the island once more, but this time they did so with increased apprehension. They were aware that they could not afford to relax their vigilance because it seemed as though every sound and movement could conceal a potential threat.

They continued their journey deeper into the island, and as they did so, they came across strange occurrences that appeared to defy explanation. They reported seeing ghostly apparitions, hearing voices that did not appear to be coming from any particular person, and sensing an energy in the air that seemed to be pulsing with a tremendous amount of power.

McCallister and his crew continued on their journey in spite of the risk. They were so intent on discovering the island's mysteries that they were willing to test their luck in order to do so.

At last, they came across a collection of ruins, which were ancient buildings that had been hidden from view by the sand for a number of years. During their exploration of the ruins, they began to find clues that led them to believe that the story of the curse was based on fact rather than legend.

They found artifacts that seemed to hold a terrible power, as well as carvings on the walls that depicted an ancient tribe's demise, and they found the carvings.

As they proceeded further into the ruins, they came across a room that was unlike any other one that they had previously explored. The walls were covered in intricate carvings, and the air was thick with an energy that didn't make any sense.

McCallister moved towards the chamber's focal point, which was a pedestal in the middle of the space. A small gemstone had been placed on the pedestal; this was the same gemstone that had been the cause of the demise of the ancient people group.

McCallister attempted to grab the gemstone, but as soon as his fingers made contact with it, he felt a jolt of electricity shoot through his body. He quickly withdrew his hand. He took a few steps backwards, and as he did, the precious stone tumbled to the ground.

A deafening roar suddenly filled the air and filled every space in it. The ground beneath them shook, and the walls of the room began to shake as well. McCallister was aware that their actions had caused the gods to become enraged, and that the curse was about to be visited upon them as a result.

They bolted from the ruins, their hearts thumping frantically in their chests as they ran. They were aware that they were running out of time as they watched the mist and darkness encircle them, and they fought to keep their focus.

After that, however, an odd thing started to take place. Both the mist and the darkness started to lift as the day continued to get brighter. The ground finally stopped shaking, and there was a noticeable increase in the amount of energy visible throughout the island.

The expressions on everyone in McCallister's crew were ones of shock and disbelief. Had they been able to lift the curse?

As they made their way back to their ship, they couldn't help but feel both relieved and curious about what they had just experienced. They had made it through the island of the forbidden curse, and they had discovered the island's hidden treasures.

However, as they continued their journey, McCallister was aware that they had not successfully lifted the curse. He was aware that others would visit the island in the future in an effort to uncover its secrets, and the island continued to be a place shrouded in secrecy and peril.

However, they were secure for the time being. They had succeeded in overcoming the dangers they faced and were now able to share their story with others.

Chapter 3: A Desperate Journey Begins

They were aware that their journey was only beginning as Captain James McCallister and his crew sailed away from the Forbidden Island. They had uncovered the myth of the curse and had lived through its wrath, but they had also uncovered something else during their investigation.

They had dug deep into the ruins of the ancient tribe, and there they discovered a map. A map that led to a location that had been forgotten for a very long time, but which was rumored to be the location of the key to unfathomable power.

McCallister was aware that in order to decipher the map's mysteries, he needed to proceed in the direction that it pointed. However, he was also aware that the journey would be difficult and fraught with danger, and that he would require as much assistance as he could get.

He turned to look at his team, his eyes glistening with enthusiasm and determination.

"We have found a map, a map that could lead us to a place of incredible power," he said. "We are very excited about this." However, the trip will be challenging and fraught with peril, and we will require as much assistance as we can get.

The crew members exchanged nervous glances with one another. They were aware of the dangers that were present on the Forbidden Island, and they realized that this journey would be even more dangerous.

On the other hand, they were conscious of the fact that they could not miss this chance. It would have been foolish to pass up the opportunity to find a location that contained unfathomable power.

As a result, they set sail once more, the location of their final destination being a mystery but their resolve remaining unshaken.

Storm after storm greeted them as they continued their journey at sea. The sails were being torn apart by the strong winds, and the ship was being pummeled by the waves, both of which threatened to sink the vessel.

However, McCallister and his crew did not let this deter them in any way. They fought their way through the storms, focusing their attention on the map that was spread out in front of them.

They had been at sea for several weeks before finally arriving at their destination. It was a tiny island, barely visible on the horizon, but they quickly realized that it was unlike any other island they had ever seen before.

The island was entirely covered in a thick jungle, and the air was heavy with the aroma of fresh flowers and fruit. They were being subjected to a severe amount of heat from the sun, which was shining brilliantly in the clear blue sky above them.

However, as they approached the shore, they became aware of an impending threat that lay just below the water's surface. They sensed that they were not alone on the island because it exuded a peculiar energy and it seemed to be alive.

They ventured deeper into the island's interior by following the map as it led them deeper into the island's jungle. The jungle was dense and inaccessible, with the tangled branches of the trees obstructing any view of the sky above.

As they ventured deeper into the jungle, they ran into a variety of strange creatures as well as obstacles along the way. They had to battle their way through dangerous terrain and avoid being attacked by vicious beasts in order to succeed.

McCallister and his crew continued on their journey in spite of the risk. They were certain that they were on the verge of making a discovery of truly extraordinary proportions, and they were determined to see it through to its conclusion.

At long last, they emerged into an open area. Ancient and festooned with moss and vines, the temple dominated the open space in the middle of the clearing.

As they got closer to the temple, they became aware of a peculiar energy that seemed to be emanating from it. They were aware that they had stumbled upon something truly remarkable because the air was thick with a sense of mystery and wonder and they had found it.

When they entered the temple, they were shocked by what they saw inside. It took their breath away. It was a room packed with priceless artifacts and relics, each one more incredible than the one before it.

They were so close to touching the treasure when they suddenly heard a sound that made their blood run cold. It was the sound of footsteps, footsteps that were approaching at an ever-increasing speed.

They turned to see a group of men who were armed and approaching them in a potentially dangerous manner. They had traveled all this way to seize the treasure for themselves, and they had no intention of allowing McCallister and his crew to get in their way.

And with that, an arduous journey got under way.

Chapter 4: A Race Against Time

When McCallister and his crew entered the temple and came face to face with the armed men already there, they realized that they were in for a fight. The men were ruthless and determined in their pursuit of the treasure, and they were willing to do anything to secure it for themselves.

After drawing their weapons, McCallister and the rest of his crew got ready to defend themselves. They could feel the weight of the moment pressing down on them, and the air itself was tense to the point that it was difficult to breathe.

After that, there was complete and utter chaos. The men charged them, their weapons shining brightly in the dim light of the temple as they did so. They fought back with everything they had, their blades flashing through the air as McCallister and his crew engaged in the conflict.

The fight was vicious and fiercely contested. Even though they were outnumbered, McCallister and his crew fought with a ferocity that could only come from desperation.

The conflict was over at last, having lasted for what seemed like an eternity. In spite of their wounds, McCallister and his team were able to emerge victorious from the conflict.

As soon as they were able to catch their breath, they had the realization that they had not escaped the ordeal unscathed. They could see that the temple had been damaged during the battle, and as a result, the structure had become unstable.

They were aware that they had to leave the temple immediately and begin their fast. They gathered as much treasure as they could carry out of the temple, and then with their hearts pounding in their chests, they made their way out.

As soon as they emerged from the temple, they could see that the jungle was full of potentially harmful elements. They were aware that the men they had fought previously had allies and that those allies would be coming after them.

They turned their attention to the environment around them as they made their way deeper into the jungle. They were aware that they needed to leave the island as soon as possible and that time was of the essence.

They navigated their way through the jungle while avoiding traps and defending themselves against dangerous creatures. They were conscious of the fact that time was running out, and they were acutely aware of the pressure that the ticking clock was exerting on their bodies.

At long last, they were able to walk out onto the beach. They were able to make out their ship off in the distance, so they knew they were getting closer to a safe haven.

Then, however, they became aware of the sound of footsteps approaching from behind them. As they turned around to face the armed men, the look of rage and desperation spread across their faces.

They were aware that they needed to move quickly. The members of McCallister's crew readied their weapons, prepared to engage in one final battle.

However, after that, an odd occurrence took place. They noticed that the air around them was beginning to shimmer, and they could sense that the island was emitting some kind of strange energy.

They were all of a sudden engulfed in a dazzling light that was all around them. McCallister and his crew were lifted off the ground as the men who had been chasing after them were carried away by the energy.

They were back on their ship when they opened their eyes after being unconscious for some time. They could make out the island in the distance, but it was getting smaller and smaller until it was completely obscured by the mist.

They were aware that the mysterious power of the island was responsible for saving their lives, and this knowledge filled them with awe and wonder. They had been on a journey of last resort, but they had emerged from it with something that was more valuable than any treasure.

They had succeeded in figuring out the island's mysteries, and they were still alive to tell the story.

Chapter 5: The Island's Many Secrets

As Captain McCallister and the rest of his crew sailed away from the mysterious island, they were all aware that they had made a discovery of truly astounding proportions. The island had been a place of mysteries and peril, but it was also a place of mystery and discovery for those who explored it.

They invested a considerable amount of time and effort into deciphering the mysteries surrounding the ancient people and the cause of their demise by poring over the artifacts and treasures that they had acquired.

They began to unearth many of the island's mysteries as they continued their research on the artifacts. They discovered ancient texts that spoke of powerful magic and long-lost civilizations, as well as artifacts that held incredible levels of power in their possession.

However, in addition to that, they found something else. They found out that the power of the island was not only contained within its artifacts and ruins, but that the island itself was alive and pulsing with an unfamiliar energy.

As they progressed further into uncovering the island's mysteries, they started to encounter some peculiar occurrences. They reported seeing apparitions, hearing voices that were not associated with any particular body part, and sensing an energy in the environment that defied explanation.

They were aware that they had made an incredible discovery, and they were intent on learning everything there was to know about it.

They went back to the island multiple times, delving deeper into its lore each time and discovering new secrets about its history each time.

They came across strange creatures and challenges, but that didn't stop them from maintaining their sense of wonder and excitement the entire time.

They came across some ruins and artifacts that were beyond extraordinary in comparison to anything else they had ever seen before. They discovered remnants of long-forgotten civilizations and magical arts, and at the same time, they felt the island's potent energy coursing through their veins.

During the course of their exploration of the island, they came across a new discovery. They made the startling discovery that the island was not only a place of wonder and discovery, but also a place of peril.

They ran into rival explorers as well as dangerous beasts, and they were forced to fight for their survival on multiple occasions.

But despite everything, they never stopped being curious and lost none of their sense of wonder. They were well aware that the island possessed an extraordinary amount of power and potential, and as a result, they were resolved to discover all of its hidden mysteries.

As a result, they carried on with their investigations, unearthings, and discoveries. They were aware that the island would forever be a place shrouded in mystery and fraught with peril, but they also were aware that it was a location rich with extraordinary opportunities.

For McCallister and the rest of his crew, the Forbidden Island would forever have a unique and significant place in their hearts. It was a place filled with excitement and new knowledge that they would never forget.

Chapter 6: The Arrival of the First Obstacle

As McCallister and his crew proceeded to investigate further into the Forbidden Island, they were aware that they were moving through potentially hazardous territory. They knew that in order to find what they were looking for on the island, which was rife with mysteries and peril, they would have to overcome a great deal of resistance.

However, they were unprepared for the arrival of the first challenge, and it manifested itself in a manner that they had not anticipated.

They were out on the water navigating their way along the coast of the island when they spotted a ship off in the distance. When they first saw it, they speculated that it might be another explorer, but as it got closer, they realized that it was actually something completely different.

They weren't familiar with the flag that was flying from the ship, and they could tell that it was well armed from what they could see. They were aware that they were going to get into some trouble.

McCallister gave the order for his crew to get ready for battle, but as the other ship approached theirs, they saw something that caused their blood to turn ice cold.

A woman who was both fierce and beautiful stood on the deck of the other ship. She wore all black, had a sword at her side, and possessed a menacing look in her eye.

She stated that her name was Captain Elizabeth Black, and that she was a notorious pirate who had made a name for herself on the open ocean. She warned McCallister and his crew that they were intruding on her territory and that they would be held accountable for the consequences of their actions.

McCallister was well aware that he was currently in a precarious situation. He had no desire to engage in combat with the captain of the pirate ship, but he also couldn't allow her to seize control of the island and all of its mysteries.

He attempted to persuade her with reason, but she would not budge from her position. She revealed to him that she had spent years looking for the island, and that once she found it, she would do anything to get her hands on the treasures that it held.

A conflict broke out as a result. The two ships collided, causing their cannons to roar and their crews to fight viciously against one another.

It was a vicious battle, and McCallister and his crew were not only outmatched in terms of numbers but also in terms of weapons. However, they did not give up and fought with all of their strength to protect both their ship and the secrets that the island held.

The conflict came to a head at what seemed like the end of several hours. McCallister and his crew were able to emerge victorious, despite having sustained significant casualties.

While they were picking up the pieces and tending to their wounds, McCallister couldn't help but wonder what other challenges were in store for them in the future. He was well aware that the island contained a great deal of peril and that there were many people who would do anything to gain access to its secrets.

However, he was also aware that he and his team were capable of rising to the occasion. They were resolute in their goal of discovering the island's mysteries, and they weren't going to let anything stand in their way.

Chapter 7: The Search for Clues

McCallister and his crew realized after their run-in with Captain Elizabeth Black and her pirate crew that they needed to exercise an even higher degree of caution in their exploration of the island in order to uncover its hidden mysteries. They were resolute in their pursuit of discovering everything that the island had to offer, but they were also aware that they could not do so on their own.

They started looking for hints, looking for anything that might point them in the direction of the next discovery. They searched through the ancient ruins and artifacts on the island thoroughly for any indication that they might have found what they were looking for.

They invested a lot of time and effort into studying old maps and texts in an effort to solve the mysteries surrounding the island. They found hidden corridors and rooms that were even more mysterious than the ones they had previously found.

However, despite all of their efforts, they were not any closer to discovering the real mysteries that lay hidden on the island. They were aware that they needed a different strategy, as well as a new point of view, in order to be able to view things in a different light.

And then they were introduced to her. She went by the name Sofia, and she was very knowledgeable about mythology and ancient languages. She had been brought on board by McCallister's patron to assist in the investigation into the mysteries surrounding the island.

They started to find clues that had been hiding in plain sight, and Sofia was a big help in the process. They found out that the island contained a great deal of potent magic and that the ancient people who had once lived there were the keepers of that magic.

They learned about the calamity that had befallen the tribe, as well as the curse that had been placed upon the island. They started to view the island in a new light, as a place that possessed an incredible amount of power and potential.

After that, they made a startling discovery that was truly extraordinary. They discovered a secret chamber that was full of artifacts, each one possessing incredible power and shrouded in more mystery than the one before it.

There were amulets that could bestow unfathomable power upon whoever wore them, and there were staffs that could call forth the elements. There were rings that could render their wearers invisible, and there were talismans that could heal wounds.

As they proceeded with their exploration of the chamber, they could sense the power of the island pulsing all around them. They were aware that they had stumbled upon something truly remarkable, something that would alter the path that they would take for the remainder of their search.

The investigation into possible hints then proceeded. As McCallister, Sofia, and the rest of the crew investigated the mysteries of the island in greater and greater depth, they uncovered secrets that had been kept a secret for centuries.

They were aware that there were still a lot of challenges to overcome, as well as the fact that there were other people who would do anything to get their hands on the island's secrets. However, they were also aware that they had the power of the island on their side, and that they were closer than they had ever been to discovering the true secrets that lay hidden on the Forbidden Island.

Chapter 8: An Unexpected Ally

They were aware that they were not the only people on the island as McCallister and his crew continued their search for the secrets of the Forbidden Island. There were others who were also exploring the island in hopes of discovering its mysteries, and not all of them were friendly.

But then they ran into someone they weren't expecting to see. It was a woman, and she was cloaked in a slender emerald robe. At the edge of the jungle, she was standing there, watching them with an inquisitive expression on her face.

McCallister and his crew approached her warily because they did not know what to expect when they got close to her. As they got closer, however, they were able to see that she posed no danger to them.

She told them her name was Melinda and that she was a sorceress who had been brought to the island by the potent magic that was present there. She shared with them that she had spent many years looking for clues on the island and that she was willing to assist them in their mission to uncover its mysteries.

At first, McCallister and his crew approached the sorceress with a healthy amount of trepidation. They were wary of her because they had heard tales of powerful magic and dangerous spells, and they did not know whether or not they could put their faith in her.

However, as they continued to talk with her, they started to realize that she was unique. She was sweet and gentle, and it appeared that she genuinely wanted to assist them in discovering the mysteries of the island.

As a result, they came to the conclusion that they should accept her offer. They invited her to accompany them in their search, and she enthusiastically accepted their invitation.

They were successful in unearthing even more of the island's hidden mysteries with Melinda's assistance. She taught them ancient spells and incantations and assisted them in releasing the hidden potential of the artifacts that were found on the island.

However, as they delved deeper into the mysteries of the island, they realized that there was something else going on at the same time. They were sensing a sense of peril that they had not been exposed to before in the form of a shadowy energy that was gathering around them.

They were aware of the necessity to exercise caution and to maintain a heightened state of alertness at all times. But in addition to that, they were aware that they had a friend in Melinda and that she would assist them in any way that she could.

As a result, the expedition to uncover the island's mysteries continued, with McCallister, his crew, and Melinda cooperating with one another in order to learn more about the Forbidden Island's hidden potential.

Chapter 9: The First Showdown

As McCallister, his crew, and Melinda continued their search for the secrets held by the Forbidden Island, they were aware that they were getting closer and closer to a significant discovery. They were aware that they were not the only ones there because they could feel the island's power pulsing all around them.

After that, the event took place. They had just begun to explore a cave that was located deep within the island's interior when they were ambushed by a group of armed men. The men appeared to be after something very specific, and they possessed a fierce and determined demeanor.

After drawing their weapons, McCallister and the rest of his crew got ready to defend themselves. Melinda took a step back, keeping her magic at the ready in case it was required.

The fight was vicious and fiercely contested. Even though they were outnumbered, McCallister and his crew fought with a ferocity that could only come from desperation.

The conflict was over at last, having lasted for what seemed like an eternity. In spite of their wounds, McCallister and his team were able to emerge victorious from the conflict.

As soon as they were able to catch their breath, they had the realization that they had not escaped the ordeal unscathed. During the conflict, they had already suffered the loss of one of their crew members, and they could see that the island was becoming even more hazardous.

On the other hand, they were aware that they were getting closer than ever before to deciphering the island's mysteries. They had been able to fend off their assailants, and in addition, they had discovered something that the men had been looking for—an ancient artifact that possessed what appeared to be an incredible amount of power.

They were aware that they needed to keep moving in order to continue their search for the island's hidden potential. As a result, they embarked on another journey, more determined than ever to learn the truth about the island and safeguard its valuables.

However, they were also aware that they could not relax their vigilance at any time. They had just come up against their first genuine challenge, and they were well aware that there were others who would do anything to seize control of the island's resources for themselves.

They continued on their journey in this manner, maintaining a state of constant vigilance and readiness for the subsequent conflict. They were well aware that they were in for a battle, but this did not deter them from their goal of achieving victory regardless of the challenges that lay in wait for them.

Chapter 10: Escaping the Danger

As McCallister and his crew continued their investigation into the mysteries surrounding the Forbidden Island, they were well aware that they were venturing into perilous territory. They had run into rival explorers, dangerous creatures, and even armed men who attacked them. All of these things had happened.

But they had never faced anything quite like the challenge that was coming up next.

They had been exploring a lengthy cave system when they came across a concealed chamber by accident. The room was packed with artifacts that possessed unfathomable levels of power; however, it also contained a great deal of peril.

As they proceeded further into the room, they tripped a trap that was set there. The ground began to shake, and the walls quickly moved in to encircle them.

There was no escape for McCallister and his crew. They looked everywhere, but there appeared to be no way out, and they were aware that time was running out.

After that, Melinda took a few steps forward. She started chanting a spell, and the movement of the walls began to slow down as a result.

Melinda kept chanting, and the walls continued to move, albeit at an increasingly slower pace. In the end, they came to a complete halt, allowing McCallister and the rest of his crew to make their getaway.

As they made their way back to their ship, they became aware of the fact that they had been placed in a more precarious situation than they had ever been in the past. They were aware, however, that they had a friend in Melinda and that the potent magic that she possessed had rescued them from an inevitable death.

They were aware that they could not relax their vigilance at any time and that they needed to be on the lookout at all times. But they also knew that they were closer than they had ever been to discovering the island's secrets, and that they had a friend in Melinda who would assist them in any way that she could. They also knew that they were closer than they had ever been to uncovering the island's secrets.

As a result, they carried on with their trip, continuing their search for the source of the Forbidden Island's true power. They were aware that danger lay ahead of them, but they were also aware that they were capable of rising to the occasion. They had the feeling that they could do anything with Melinda by their side, and they were prepared to overcome any challenges that stood in their way.

Chapter 11: The Island's Mysterious Wildlife

McCallister and his crew continued their search for the secrets of the Forbidden Island, and as they did so, they came across a number of fantastic and strange creatures. The island was teeming with life, but it also posed a significant threat to its inhabitants.

They came across monstrous spiders with bites that were poisonous, enormous snakes that could crush a man to death in a matter of seconds, and even a pack of wild dogs that had been mutated by the strange energy that emanated from the island.

However, in addition to that, they came across something else. Something that was enchanting and mysterious at the same time.

When they came across it, they were strolling along the precipice of a cliff. A beast that was unlike anything that any of them had ever seen before.

It appeared to be a bird, but it was unlike any other bird that any of them had ever seen before. It had long, graceful wings that appeared to shimmer in the sunlight, and its feathers were a brilliant shade of blue.

As they watched, the bird took off into the sky and continued its journey over the water. They could tell that it was no ordinary bird, but rather a magnificent creature that possessed both power and grace in abundance.

They were aware that they needed to find out more about the mysterious wildlife that lived on the island. Because of this, they started documenting the behaviors of the different creatures they came across and analyzing the routines they followed.

They found out that the island was inhabited by animals that were completely unique to any other species that could be found anywhere else in the world. There were enormous beetles that could lift objects that were twice their size, as well as lizards the size of mountains covered in scales that resembled armor.

However, they also found out that the wildlife on the island was not only unique and unusual, but that it was also dangerous. They ran into groups of wild animals that would attack without any prior warning, so they learned the importance of staying vigilant at all times.

But despite the risks, they couldn't take their eyes off the animals that lived on the island. They were aware that they had made an incredible discovery, and they were resolved to acquire as much information as they could regarding it.

As a result, they carried on with their journey, conducting research on the wildlife of the island, and looking for the source of the Forbidden Island's true power. They were well aware that they were in for a battle, but they were prepared to overcome any challenges that stood in their way, even if it meant going up against some of the most vicious beasts that the island had to offer.

Chapter 12: Into the Heart of Darkness

As McCallister and his crew continued their search for the secrets hidden on the Forbidden Island, they became aware that they were drawing ever closer to a significant discovery. They were aware that they were not the only ones there because they could feel the island's power pulsing all around them.

Then, they were successful in locating it. An enormous temple that is secreted away somewhere in the interior of the island. They were able to sense a power that had been around for a very long time emanating from within the temple, which was gloomy and sinister.

They were aware that they needed to investigate the temple in order to unearth its mysteries and figure out what was at the temple's core.

As they proceeded further inside the temple, they came across various puzzles and traps that appeared to be set up with the intention of excluding anyone who did not have the ability to overcome them.

But McCallister and his crew were unflappable, and they continued to make progress despite the challenges. They had to work through riddles and avoid getting caught in traps until they were finally able to enter the main part of the temple.

And there, they came across an unbelievable discovery. A vast room that was stuffed with ancient artifacts and potent magic.

They were aware that they had made an important discovery, one that had the potential to alter the way in which they conducted their investigation indefinitely.

However, as they proceeded to investigate the room further, they became aware that there was something else going on. They were sensing a sense of peril that they had not been exposed to before in the form of a shadowy energy that was gathering around them.

They were aware of the necessity to exercise caution and to maintain a heightened state of alertness at all times. But in addition to this, they were aware that they had uncovered something truly remarkable, something that would aid them in their search for the power that was hidden within the Forbidden Island.

As a result, they proceeded further and further into the interior of the island, making their way deeper and deeper into its heart. They were aware that each step brought them closer to an incredible discovery, but they also were aware that the risk they faced was growing with each step they took.

But despite the challenges that lay in wait for them, they were resolute in their pursuit of the secret behind the Forbidden Island's incredible power. They were well aware that they were in for a battle, but they were prepared to take on any difficulties that might be thrown their way, even if it meant delving even further into the depths of the underworld.

Chapter 13: The Second Obstacle Appears

They were aware that they were getting closer to the island's true power as McCallister and his crew continued their journey deeper into the heart of the Forbidden Island. They had discovered ancient artifacts and investigated the mysterious wildlife that lived on the island, and as a result, they knew that they were heading in the right direction.

However, at that point, they were confronted with their second significant obstacle. Competing explorers at the time were led by a man named Charles Drake, who was the group's leader. Drake was infamous throughout the world as a treasure hunter, and he had spent years looking for the island's hidden treasures.

McCallister and his crew were aware that they needed to exercise caution at all times. They were well aware that Drake was not someone to be trifled with and that he would stop at nothing in his pursuit of the power that the island held for himself.

As a result, they braced themselves for the worst. In preparation for a possible assault, they fortified their camp and placed traps around their various pieces of equipment.

However, they did not have to wait for very long at all. They were awakened in the late hours of one night by the sound of gunfire. They were aware that they needed to be prepared because they could hear the sounds of Drake's men coming closer to them.

The fight was vicious and fiercely contested. The men under Drake's command were resolute and well-equipped; consequently, it appeared that they held the upper hand.

On the other hand, McCallister and his companions did not give up easily. They fought back with everything they had, adamant that they would not let anyone discover the island's secrets.

The conflict was over at last, having lasted for what seemed like an eternity. In spite of their wounds, McCallister and his team were able to emerge victorious from the conflict.

As soon as they were able to catch their breath, they had the realization that they had not escaped the ordeal unscathed. During the conflict, they had suffered the loss of several members of their crew, and they could see that the island was becoming even more hazardous for them to be on.

On the other hand, they were aware that they were getting closer than ever before to deciphering the island's mysteries. They had vanquished their foes, and in addition, they had discovered something that Drake had been searching for: a map that appeared to lead to the source of the island's untapped potential.

They were aware that they needed to keep moving in order to continue their search for the island's hidden potential. As a result, they embarked on another journey, more determined than ever to learn the truth about the island and safeguard its valuables.

However, they were also aware that they could not relax their vigilance at any time. They had just come up against their second genuine challenge, and they were well aware that there were others who would do anything to seize the island's power for themselves.

They continued on their journey in this manner, maintaining a state of constant vigilance and readiness for whatever the next challenge might be. They were well aware that they were in for a battle, but this did not deter them from their goal of achieving victory regardless of the obstacles that lay in wait for them.

Chapter 14: Uncovering the Island's Dark History

They were aware that they were getting closer to the island's true power as McCallister and his crew continued their search for the secrets of the Forbidden Island. They had prevailed over other explorers as well as dangerous creatures, and they had discovered artifacts that possessed incredible power.

However, they were also aware that there was something else going on at the same time. Something that they had not discovered up to that point.

As a result, they started digging further into the history of the island in order to discover its mysteries and acquire additional information regarding its murky background.

They found out that the island had been inhabited by a powerful civilization in the past, one that had exploited the island's magic to accomplish extraordinary things while it was their home. They had constructed enormous temples and colossal statues, and they had been leaders in both the field of magic and the field of technology.

But then, there was an issue with something. The once-thriving civilization was now in ruins, and the once-peaceful island had descended into a place of darkness and peril.

McCallister and his crew began to uncover an increasing number of the island's mysteries as they dug deeper into the island's history. They uncovered ancient texts and maps, which allowed them to put together the history of the island in a piecemeal fashion.

They found out that the island had been cursed, and that its power had been tainted by a malevolent force that had been released upon the world as a result of the arrogance of the civilization.

However, they also discovered that there was a method to lift the island's enchantment, thereby releasing its latent potential and restoring it to its former glory.

And with that, they got to work on making it happen. They used the ancient maps as guides and deciphered the ancient texts in order to find what they were looking for in the end.

An enormous temple that is secreted away somewhere in the interior of the island. There was a temple on the island that held the secret to removing the spell and releasing the island's latent potential.

They were aware that the journey they were about to embark on would be risky and that they would be confronted with obstacles that they could not even begin to imagine. But they were resolved to see it through to the end, to discover the secrets of the island, and to bring the island's power back into the light.

As a result, they proceeded further and further into the interior of the Forbidden Island, making their way ever closer to its center. They were aware that they were drawing closer to the source of the island's true power, and they were resolved to discover it regardless of the challenges that lay in wait for them.

Chapter 15: A Deadly Trap

They were aware that they were getting closer to the island's true power as McCallister and his crew continued their journey deeper into the heart of the Forbidden Island. They had prevailed over other explorers as well as dangerous creatures, and they had discovered artifacts that possessed incredible power. They had even discovered the dark history of the island and learned how to free it from the curse that had been placed upon it.

But then, they ran into a trap that would prove fatal. They were making their way through a constricted area when all of a sudden, the ground beneath them gave way, and they fell into a large hole.

They were aware that they needed to find a way out of the pit before it was too late because it was filled with spikes that could kill them.

As they looked for a way out of the situation, they became aware that they were not the only ones there. They were aware that they were in an increasingly precarious situation because they could hear the sound of someone approaching them.

It was Drake and the men under his command. They had been following McCallister and his crew for some time, patiently waiting for the right moment to make their move.

McCallister and his crew were aware that they needed to exercise caution at all times. They were well aware that Drake was not someone to be trifled with and that he would stop at nothing in his pursuit of the power that the island held for himself.

However, they were also aware that they needed to get out of the pit as quickly as possible.

They pooled their resources and came up with creative solutions to solve the problem by working together. They were able to climb up the walls of the pit and get away from the dangerous spikes that were below them.

But despite this, they were still forced to contend with Drake and his men.

The fight was vicious and fiercely contested. The men under Drake's command were resolute and well-equipped; consequently, it appeared that they held the upper hand.

On the other hand, McCallister and his companions did not give up easily. They fought back with everything they had, adamant that they would not let anyone discover the island's secrets.

The conflict was over at last, having lasted for what seemed like an eternity. In spite of their wounds, McCallister and his team were able to emerge victorious from the conflict.

As soon as they were able to catch their breath, they had the realization that they had not escaped the ordeal unscathed. During the conflict, they had suffered the loss of several members of their crew, and they could see that the island was becoming even more hazardous for them to be on.

On the other hand, they were aware that they were getting closer than ever before to deciphering the island's mysteries. They had vanquished their foes, and they had uncovered something that Drake had been searching for: a clue that appeared to lead to the island's true power. Both of these victories were significant.

They were aware that they needed to keep moving in order to continue their search for the island's hidden potential. As a result, they embarked on another journey, this time with the purpose of discovering the island's mysteries and safeguarding its treasures.

However, they were also aware that they could not relax their vigilance at any time. They had fallen victim to yet another lethal trap,

THE FORBIDDEN ISLAND: A RACE AGAINST TIME

and they were well aware that there were others on the island who would do anything to seize control of its resources for themselves.

They continued on their journey in this manner, staying vigilant and alert at all times, and always being prepared for the next potentially lethal trap. They were well aware that they were in for a battle, but this did not deter them from their goal of achieving victory regardless of the obstacles that lay in wait for them.

Chapter 16: Fighting for Survival

As McCallister and his crew continued their search for the true power that lay within the Forbidden Island, they were aware that they were getting closer than they had ever been before. They had prevailed over other rival explorers, dangerous creatures, and lethal traps, and they had discovered clues that appeared to lead to the source of the island's true power.

However, they were also aware that they were about to engage in the battle of their lives.

They could feel the darkness closing in on them as the island's perilous conditions continued to worsen. They were in a battle for their lives, and they were well aware that they could not relax their defenses at any point.

They were ambushed by additional lethal traps, and they fought off additional adversarial explorers. They came across new types of animals, ones that they had never encountered before, and they quickly realized that they were in over their heads.

However, they were also aware that they could not give up at this point. They realized that they had come too far to turn back now and that they had no choice but to see it through to its conclusion.

After that, they came up against the last of the challenges. A gigantic beast that was unlike anything they had ever encountered before. It had enormous claws that were as sharp as razors, and its teeth were like daggers.

They were aware that they were about to engage in the most important battle of their lives. They had never come up against anything as ferocious and relentless as the creature before, and they had no idea what to expect.

On the other hand, McCallister and his companions did not give up easily. They fought back with everything they had, employing every strategy and method that they had picked up on their travels as they went along.

The fight was vicious and fiercely contested. The beast was formidable in its strength and power, and it appeared to be gaining the upper hand at this point.

On the other hand, McCallister and his companions did not give up easily. They fought back with everything that they had, determined to protect the secrets of the island and come out on top.

The battle came to an end after what seemed like an eternity, with McCallister and his team emerging victorious despite being bloodied and battered in the process.

As they paused to catch their breath, they came to the conclusion that they had, in fact, located what they had been looking for all along. The real power of the Forbidden Island, a power that had been concealed for hundreds of years.

They were aware that they had stumbled upon something truly remarkable, something that had the potential to alter the path that history would take.

They were worn out but victorious when they finally made it back to their ship. They were well aware that they had been successful in accomplishing something truly remarkable, and they were resolved to keep the island's secrets safe for future generations.

They had engaged in combat to ensure their continued existence, and they had emerged victorious. They were aware that the trip had been challenging, but they also knew that it had been worthwhile to make the effort.

They eventually left the Forbidden Island, sailing away with the knowledge that they had been a part of something truly remarkable during their time there. They had found the key to unlocking the island's latent potential, and as a result, they emerged victorious from the struggle for survival.

Chapter 17: A Glimmer of Hope

The realization dawned on McCallister and his crew as they sailed away from the Forbidden Island that they had just accomplished something truly remarkable hit them as they sailed away. They had found the key to unlocking the island's latent potential, and as a result, they emerged victorious from the struggle for survival.

However, they were also aware that their journey had not yet come to an end. They were obligated to guard the island's secrets and make certain that its genuine power was not abused in any way.

They were off in the distance when they noticed something on the horizon. A glimmer of hope, a sign that there was more to their journey than they had initially thought, it was just enough to make them want to keep going.

It was a group of travelers, people who were interested in hearing more about their journey because they had heard about it. They were interested in exploring the island so that they could witness the island's power for themselves.

McCallister and his crew were well aware of the obligation placed on them to keep the island's secrets secure. They had uncovered something that was truly remarkable, but they couldn't let it get into the wrong hands for fear of it being used against them.

As a result, they had a conversation with the travelers. They described their journey to them, including the challenges they had to overcome and the threats they had come across along the way.

But they also told them about the island's true power and the incredible magic that lay at its core. This was one of the things they told them about the island.

The travelers paid attention, and after hearing what was said, they were aware that they needed to be cautious. They were aware that the island posed a threat, and they were also aware that there were those who would resort to any means necessary in order to seize control of its power.

However, they were also aware that there was still a chance. They were aware that it was possible to harness the island's true power for the greater good and that this power could be put to use to make the world a better place.

As a result, they embarked on their own adventure, bound and determined to discover everything there was to know about the island.

As McCallister and his crew watched the departing travelers sail away, they were conscious of the fact that they had successfully transferred the responsibility of keeping the island's secrets to a subsequent generation.

They were aware that the journey that lay ahead of them would be challenging, and that there would be difficulties and roadblocks that the travelers had not yet encountered.

However, they were also aware that there was still a chance. They had succeeded in uncovering the true power that the Forbidden Island possessed, and they had communicated this information to those who were able to carry on their work.

And with that, they set sail, content in the knowledge that they had just been a part of something truly remarkable. They had reached the point where they knew everything there was to know about the Forbidden Island, and they had given the responsibility of keeping those secrets safe to the following generation.

Chapter 18: The Third Obstacle Looms

When the adventurers set sail for the Forbidden Island, they did so with the knowledge that they were about to embark on a challenging trip. They were aware that in order to succeed, just like McCallister and his crew, they would need to overcome the challenges and perils that they themselves would encounter because they had heard about those experiences.

Next, they were confronted with the third and most significant challenge. It was an enormous storm, unlike anything that any of them had ever encountered before. They were aware that they were going to be engaged in combat due to the fact that the winds howled and the rain came down in sheets.

However, they were also aware that they needed to exercise caution. They were aware that the storm posed a threat, and that it was possible for them to be blown off course or even shipwrecked.

They came up with a plan to get through the storm by working together and putting all of their heads together. They fought against the wind and the rain, making it difficult for them to steer their ship in the right direction.

However, they were also aware that there was something else going on at the same time. They were able to sense an odd energy in the air, a power that gave off the impression that it was coming directly from the island.

They were aware that they were drawing nearer to the source of the island's true power, and they were also aware that they needed to press on regardless of the difficulties that lay in wait for them in the future.

After what seemed like hours had passed, the storm finally started to let up. They emerged bloodied and battered, but they were aware that they had prevailed over yet another significant challenge.

However, they were also aware that there were additional difficulties to come. They were aware that they needed to be cautious because they had heard rumors about the mysterious wildlife that lived on the island.

After that, they came across something that had never appeared in front of them before. It was a gigantic beast, unlike anything that any of them had ever witnessed before. They knew they were in over their heads when they saw that it had multiple heads and claws that were as sharp as razors.

However, they were also aware that they could not give up at this point. They realized that they had come too far to turn back now and that they had no choice but to see it through to its conclusion.

As a result, they banded together and employed all of their respective abilities and strategies in order to vanquish the beast. They fought against its many heads and sharp claws, struggling to defend themselves and their ship from the creature's attacks.

At long last, after what seemed like countless hours of struggle, they emerged victorious. They had triumphed over the beast, but they were well aware that there would be additional obstacles to overcome.

They were aware that they were drawing nearer to the source of the island's true power, and they were also aware that they had to proceed forward regardless of the challenges that lay in wait for them.

They continued on their journey in this manner, maintaining a state of constant vigilance and readiness for the subsequent challenge they would face. They were well aware that they were in for a battle, but this did not deter them from their goal of achieving victory regardless of the obstacles that lay in wait for them.

Chapter 19: The Final Battle Approaches

As the travelers progressed further into the interior of the Forbidden Island, they became aware that they were drawing ever nearer to the source of the island's mystical power. They had encountered many difficulties and setbacks, but they had persisted despite these things because they were determined to learn the island's mysteries and satisfy their natural curiosity.

After that, they were confronted with the last and most significant of their challenges. They had never seen anything quite like this enormous fortress before in their lives. They knew that in order to discover the island's true power, they would have to fight their way inside, as it was guarded by fierce warriors, and they were prepared for this challenge.

They were well aware that the decisive conflict was drawing near, and they were resolved to emerge victorious from it. They realized that they had come too far to turn back now and that they had no choice but to see it through to its conclusion.

They coordinated their efforts and used every trick and strategy in their toolbox to sneak inside the stronghold. They fought off the guards and fought their way inside, intent on discovering the island's true power and using it to their advantage.

Then, all of a sudden, they stumbled upon what it was that they had been looking for all along. The origin of the island's enchantment, the true source of its power, which had been kept a secret for centuries.

However, they were also aware that they were not the only ones there. Their adversaries, led by Drake, had followed them to the island, and once there, they made it clear that they intended to seize the power that the island possessed for themselves.

The decisive conflict was extremely violent and bloody. The rivals of the travelers engaged in a fierce battle, employing every available strategy and method throughout the course of the conflict.

But in the end, the travelers were successful as a result of their dogged determination and their willingness to cooperate with one another. They had succeeded in locating the source of the island's power and in defending it from those who would put it to harmful use.

They were well aware that they had been successful in accomplishing something truly remarkable as they sailed away from the island that was off limits to them. They had succeeded in the climactic conflict, as well as in deciphering the island's hidden mysteries, and the island had ultimately fallen into their hands.

However, they were also aware that their journey had not yet come to an end. They were responsible for keeping the island's secrets safe and preventing the island's actual power from being exploited in any way.

They then embarked on their journey, confident in their ability to disseminate the information they had learned to the rest of the world and resolved to keep the secrets of the Forbidden Island safe for future generations.

Chapter 20: The Island's Greatest Secret

As the adventurers sailed away from the island of the forbidden, they were aware that they had just completed an endeavor of truly remarkable proportions. They had been victorious in the final conflict and had discovered the secrets that the island had to offer.

However, they were also aware that it was their duty to keep the island's secrets safe and to make certain that its real power was not abused in any way.

As a result, they returned home and devoted a significant amount of time to analyzing the artifacts and data they had accumulated during their travels. They gained knowledge of the incredible magic that existed at the island's core and realized that it had the potential to be utilized for the greater good of the world.

However, they were also aware that they needed to exercise caution. They had to make sure that those who would abuse the island's true power did not get their hands on it, as they could not risk having it fall into the wrong hands.

After that, they came to an important realization. It was the greatest secret that the island could possibly keep, and it had been kept a secret for centuries.

They discovered a long-forgotten temple that was crammed with potent artifacts and a wealth of knowledge that had been missing for many years. They were well aware that this was the source of the island's true power, and as a result, they were resolved to guard it no matter what the cost.

They coordinated their efforts and pooled all of their talents and strategies in order to keep the temple and its treasures safe. They were aware that there were others who would do anything to seize its power for themselves, and as a result, they were resolute in their mission to safeguard it from those who would put it to harmful use.

After that, they came to a conclusion about what to do. They would put the island's real power to good use by making the world a better place and assisting those who are in need.

They were well aware that the journey would be challenging, and that it would be fraught with difficulties and difficulties along the way. However, they were also aware that it was their duty to make use of the island's actual power in order to effect positive change elsewhere in the world.

As a result, they embarked on a fresh adventure with the purpose of putting the island's untapped potential to good use while also preserving its mysteries for future generations.

They were well aware that they had been successful in accomplishing something truly remarkable as they sailed away from the island that was off limits to them. They had triumphed in the climactic conflict, their adversaries had been vanquished, and they had discovered the island's hidden treasures.

However, they were also aware that their journey had not yet come to an end. They had a duty to safeguard the island's mysteries from those who would exploit their power and to put the island's true potential to good use in the world.

They were eager to embark on a fresh adventure and were resolved to make a positive impact on the world. As a result, they set sail.

Chapter 21: Racing Against the Clock

The adventurers were aware that they were in a race against the clock as they set out on their new journey to harness the island's true power for the greater good. They were aware that they only had a short amount of time to make a difference in the world, and because of this, they moved as quickly as they could.

They labored without stopping, drawing on the real power of the island to cure the sick, provide food for the starving, and bring peace to those who were in need. They ventured all over the world, putting their abilities and expertise to good use in order to make a difference and to safeguard the island's secrets from those who would exploit them.

On the other hand, they were well aware that time was running out. They were aware that they could only access a certain amount of the island's true power, so they made every effort to conserve it.

After that, they came to an important realization. They discovered a way to harness the power of the island's magic and use it to create a renewable source of energy that can be used everywhere in the world.

They were aware that this was their opportunity to make a genuine difference, to alter the path that history would take, and to build a brighter future for everyone.

They were aware that they were competing against the ticking clock, however. They were aware that they could not afford to squander even a single second as they raced against the clock to develop this novel source of energy.

As a result, they toiled away without stopping, harnessing the island's latent potential to develop a reliable supply of energy for the rest of the world. They traversed the globe, collaborating with various governments and organizations to develop and implement this innovative technology, all the while ensuring that the island's secrets remained safe from those who would exploit them.

After that, they were successful in achieving their objective. They had succeeded in developing a renewable source of energy, one that would alter the path that history would take and make the future a better place for everyone.

They were well aware that they had been successful in accomplishing something truly remarkable as they sailed away from the island that was off limits to them. They had put the island's true power to good use, and as a result, the world now has a future that is more environmentally friendly.

However, they were also aware that their journey had not yet come to an end. They were responsible for keeping the island's secrets safe and preventing the island's real power from being exploited in any way, shape, or form.

And so it came to pass that they set sail, eager to embark on a fresh adventure and resolute to keep the secrets of the Forbidden Island safe for future generations.

Chapter 22: The Tides Turn

As the travelers continued their quest to safeguard the secrets of the island, they were well aware that they would encounter a number of difficulties and impediments along the way. They had already encountered a great deal of difficulty, but they were resolved to see the process through to its conclusion.

After that, they were confronted with a fresh obstacle. It was a group of individuals who were aware of the real power that the island possessed and desired to exploit it for their own benefit.

They were aware that these individuals posed a threat, and they were also aware that they needed to move quickly in order to safeguard the island's secrets.

They coordinated their efforts and shared all of the information and expertise that they possessed in order to keep the island's secrets safe and prevent them from falling into the wrong hands.

After that, an extraordinary occurrence took place. Eventually, the tides changed, and those individuals who had previously sought to abuse the island's genuine power started to see the error of their ways.

They came to the conclusion that the only way to harness the island's full potential and use it to do good in the world and build a brighter future for everyone was to put it to constructive use.

They did this by allying themselves with the voyagers and cooperating with them in an effort to keep the island's secrets safe and to put the island's true power to good use.

The adventurers were aware that they had just completed an endeavor of truly remarkable proportions as they made their way away from the island of the Forbidden. They had preserved the island's mysteries and put the island's untapped potential to good use.

However, they were also aware that their journey had not yet come to an end. They were tasked with the duty of preserving the island's mysteries for future generations and seeing to it that the island's untapped potential was only put to beneficial use.

As a result, they embarked on a fresh adventure, determined to leave their mark on the world while also ensuring that the secrets of the Forbidden Island are preserved for future generations.

Chapter 23: The End is Near

As the travelers continued their journey to safeguard the secrets of the island, they were aware that they were drawing closer and closer to the destination. Even though they had made so much progress, they were well aware that their work was not yet finished.

After that, a message was delivered to them. It was a warning that an unauthorized group of individuals had found the location of the Forbidden Island and were making preparations to invade it.

They were aware that they needed to move quickly in order to keep the island's secrets safe and to avoid the possibility of those secrets falling into the wrong hands.

They labored nonstop, drawing on the entirety of their experience and expertise, in order to keep the island and its mysteries safe. They conducted research and made preparations in anticipation of the impending invasion.

After that, the day finally came. The invading forces made it to the shores of the Forbidden Island, where they prepared to seize the island's untapped potential for themselves.

On the other hand, they were met with ferocious opposition. The explorers and their allies fought valiantly, utilizing all of their abilities and the information they had acquired, in order to safeguard the island and the secrets it held.

After what seemed like hours of constant conflict, the intruders were ultimately victorious. After a hard-fought battle, the travelers and their allies emerged victorious, having preserved the island's mysteries as well as its inherent strength.

The adventurers were aware that they had just completed an endeavor of truly remarkable proportions as they made their way away from the island of the Forbidden. They had preserved the island's mysteries and put the island's untapped potential to good use.

On the other hand, they were aware that their journey had come to an end. They had finished everything that they had planned to do, and they were well aware that it was now time to move on to other things.

They eventually departed the Forbidden Island, leaving it in their wake as they sailed away. They were confident that its lore would not be compromised and that its underlying strength would be put to beneficial use.

They were well aware that they had been a part of something truly remarkable as they set sail in the opposite direction. They had left their mark on the world, and they had ensured that the mysteries of the Forbidden Island would be safeguarded for future generations.

Chapter 24: A Heroic Sacrifice

As the adventurers sailed away from the island of the forbidden, they were aware that they had just completed an endeavor of truly remarkable proportions. They had preserved the island's mysteries and put the island's untapped potential to good use.

On the other hand, they were aware that there had been a cost involved. One of their own had bravely laid down their life for the cause, giving up their life in order to keep the island's secrets safe and to make sure that its real power was not abused.

They grieved their loss, but at the same time, they were aware that the sacrifice they had made had not been in vain. They were aware that their fallen comrade would be pleased with how they had handled the situation, as they had kept the island's secrets safe and put the island's true power to good use.

After that, another message arrived at their doorstep. It was a warning that a new group of people had found out where the Forbidden Island was located and were planning to invade it.

They were aware that they needed to move quickly in order to keep the island's secrets safe and to avoid the possibility of those secrets falling into the wrong hands once more.

However, they were also aware that they could not complete the task on their own. They were in need of assistance, and they were confident that they could rely on their allies.

They put in countless hours of labor in order to assemble their support network and get ready for the impending invasion. They were aware that the stakes were significantly higher this time around.

After that, the day finally came. The invading forces made it to the shores of the Forbidden Island, where they prepared to seize the island's untapped potential for themselves.

However, the travelers and their allies were well prepared for this encounter. They fought valiantly, employing all of their abilities and the wealth of knowledge they possessed, to preserve the island and its mysteries.

After what seemed like hours of constant conflict, the intruders were ultimately victorious. On the other hand, there was no heroic sacrifice made this time.

The adventurers were aware that they had just completed an endeavor of truly remarkable proportions as they made their way away from the island of the Forbidden. They had been successful in preserving the island's mysteries and in harnessing its latent potential for the common good, and they had done so with no additional casualties.

They were aware that their journey was at an end, and that they could now get some much-needed rest. They had finished everything that they had set out to do, and they were confident that the secrets of the Forbidden Island would be preserved for future generations.

As they sailed away, they were confident in the knowledge that they had contributed to positive change in the world and that their slain comrade would be pleased with their accomplishments. They had preserved the mysteries of the Forbidden Island, and they had put the island's untapped potential to good use.

Chapter 25: A Narrow Escape

As the adventurers sailed away from the island of the forbidden, they were aware that they had just completed an endeavor of truly remarkable proportions. They had preserved the island's mysteries and put the island's untapped potential to good use.

However, they were also aware that their journey had not yet come to an end. They had to watch out for anyone who might steal the island's secrets or abuse its real strength in order to fulfill their mission.

They were then issued a second cautionary statement. Someone or some people had figured out the location of the Forbidden Island, and they were making preparations to colonize it once more.

They were aware that they needed to move quickly in order to keep the island's secrets safe and to avoid the possibility of those secrets falling into the wrong hands once more.

They put in countless hours of labor in order to assemble their support network and get ready for the impending invasion. They were aware that the stakes were significantly higher this time around.

After that, the day finally came. The invading forces made it to the shores of the Forbidden Island, where they prepared to seize the island's untapped potential for themselves.

However, the travelers and their allies were well prepared for this encounter. They fought valiantly, employing all of their abilities and the wealth of knowledge they possessed, to preserve the island and its mysteries.

After what seemed like hours of constant conflict, the intruders were ultimately victorious. However, as the travelers were getting ready to embark on their journey, they came to the realization that they were not yet safe.

One of the invaders managed to get away, and now he was focused on seizing the real power that the island possessed for himself. He had made off with one of the island's artifacts, a potent amulet that had the potential to be used to tap into the island's magical energy.

The travelers were aware that time was of the essence and needed to move quickly. They gave chase to the intruder, intent on preventing him from abusing the real power of the island in any way he could.

They were able to locate him on a small island that he had chosen to use as a staging area for his operations. They were aware that they needed to move quickly in order to prevent him from using the amulet to tap into the island's magical power.

As a result, they engaged the invader in valiant combat, employing all of their resources, including their expertise and their knowledge. They were aware that the destiny of the entire world was on the line and that they could not afford to let him win.

They prevailed in the end, despite the arduous fight that had been waged. They were successful in preventing the invader from abusing the real power of the island, and they shielded the rest of the world from the threats that the island posed.

The adventurers were aware that they had just completed an endeavor of truly remarkable significance as they sailed away from the secluded island. They were able to keep the island's secrets safe, put its real power to good use, and prevent others from abusing it in the process.

However, they were also aware that their journey had not yet come to an end. They had a duty to keep the island's secrets safe for future generations, and they had to make sure that its real power was never abused in the future.

As a result, they boarded a boat and sailed away, confident that they would continue their journey and keep the secrets of the Forbidden Island safe for future generations.

Chapter 26: The Aftermath

As the adventurers sailed away from the island of the forbidden, they were aware that they had just completed an endeavor of truly remarkable proportions. They were able to keep the island's secrets safe, put its real power to good use, and prevent others from abusing it in the process.

However, they were also aware that there would be repercussions for their actions. They were a contributing factor to the transformation that was taking place in the world.

They went all over the world, using the real power of the island to treat those who were ill, feed those who were hungry, and bring peace to those who were in need. They collaborated with various governments and international organizations to develop environmentally friendly energy sources and to defend the rest of the world against those who would exploit the island's untapped potential.

On the other hand, they were aware that there were some people who would never forget what had taken place on the Forbidden Island. They were aware that they needed to be prepared in case those individuals decided to take vengeance on them.

As a result, they braced themselves for the worst. They became skilled in both physical combat and magical arts, employing all of their acquired abilities and information in order to safeguard not only themselves but also the people they cared about.

Then the assaults began in earnest. Although they were vicious and unyielding, the travelers were well prepared for them. They fought valiantly, employing every one of their abilities and all that they had learned to shield themselves and their allies.

After what seemed like months of constant conflict, the assaults came to an end. The travelers had prevailed over their adversaries and were able to keep themselves and their allies safe from those who were out for vengeance.

As the survivors of the attacks made their way away from the devastation caused by the attacks, they were aware that they had been a part of something truly remarkable. They had been successful in preventing those who would abuse the island's true power from wreaking havoc on the world, and they had brought about change in the world.

However, they were also aware that their journey had not yet come to an end. They had a duty to keep the island's secrets safe for future generations, and they had to make sure that its real power was never abused in the future.

As a result, they boarded a boat and sailed away, confident that they would continue their journey and keep the secrets of the Forbidden Island safe for future generations. They were aware that the world was undergoing change, and they were prepared to take on any difficulties that may arise in the future.

Chapter 27: A New Dawn

As the travelers sailed away from the aftermath of the attacks, they were aware that they had achieved something truly remarkable despite the challenges they had faced. They had been successful in preventing those who would abuse the island's true power from wreaking havoc on the world, and they had brought about change in the world.

However, they were also aware that their journey had not yet come to an end. They had a duty to keep the island's secrets safe for future generations, and they had to make sure that its real power was never abused in the future.

As a result, they boarded a boat and sailed away, confident that they would continue their journey and keep the secrets of the Forbidden Island safe for future generations.

However, as they continued their journey, an extraordinary event transpired. They witnessed the world around them undergoing change, and they were aware that they had contributed to that change in some way.

The true power of the island had been tapped into, and it was now being put to use to build a brighter future for everyone. People were banding together to make a difference in the world, and sustainable energy sources were being put into practice.

After that, a message was delivered to them. It came from a group of individuals who were aware of the actual power that the island possessed and desired to put that power to good use.

They were aware that this was their opportunity to make a genuine difference, to alter the path that history would take, and to build a brighter future for everyone.

As a result, they collaborated with this fresh collection of individuals, imparting their wisdom and experience in an effort to effect positive change in the wider world. They embarked on a journey around the world with the goal of using their experience and expertise to assist those in need and to make the world a better place.

They were able to witness the start of a brand new era. Imagine a world in which the true power of the island was being used for the greater good, and in which people worked together to build a brighter future for everyone.

The travelers realized as they sailed away from the world that they had helped to create that they had achieved something truly remarkable as a result of their efforts. They had been successful in preventing those who would abuse the island's true power from wreaking havoc on the world, and they had brought about change in the world.

However, they were also aware that their journey had not yet come to an end. They had a duty to keep the island's secrets safe for future generations, and they had to make sure that its real power was never abused in the future.

As a result, they boarded a boat and sailed away, confident that they would continue their journey and keep the secrets of the Forbidden Island safe for future generations. They were aware that the world was undergoing change, and they were prepared to take on any difficulties that may arise in the future.

Chapter 28: The Journey Home

They knew that they had been a part of something truly remarkable as they sailed away from the world that they had helped to create while at the same time they were aware that they had accomplished something truly remarkable. They had been successful in preventing those who would abuse the island's true power from wreaking havoc on the world, and they had brought about change in the world.

On the other hand, they were aware that their trip was drawing to a close. They had achieved all of the goals that they had set for themselves, and it was finally time for them to head back home.

They were eager to get back to their loved ones and the lives that they had previously abandoned, and so they set sail for their homeland.

They were thinking back on their trip the whole time they were on the road. They recalled the victories that they had achieved as well as the difficulties that they had overcome and the people that they had met along the way.

And they were aware of the ways in which their trip had altered them. They had matured into a more powerful, wiser, and determined group than they had ever been before.

At long last, they caught sight of the recognizable coastline of their own country. They were greeted by their loved ones as they sailed into the harbor where they had been waiting for them.

As they disembarked from the vessel, there were happy tears and hugs shared amongst all of the passengers. Because of the sacrifices that they had made and the impact that they had made in the world, the people of their town greeted them with cheers and applause when they returned home.

As they moved through the town, they became aware of the transformations that had occurred as a direct result of their efforts. People were working together to make a difference in the world, and sustainable energy sources had been implemented.

And they were aware that their travels were not yet complete. They were obligated to continue guarding the island's secrets and to make certain that its actual power was never abused in the future.

However, for the time being, they were at home. They were aware that the world was a better place as a result of the work that they had done, which was something truly remarkable in and of itself.

As they readjusted to their previous lives, they were well aware that the journey that had led them to this point would remain ingrained in their memories forever. They had triumphed over insurmountable obstacles and emerged victorious; as a result, they were well aware that their fortitude had increased significantly.

And so it was that they lived their lives, keeping the recollections of their trip close at hand the entire time. They were aware that they had achieved something truly remarkable, and they were also aware that their journey had not yet reached its conclusion. For the time being, however, they were safe and sound in their own home.

Chapter 29: A Bittersweet Victory

As the travelers readjusted to their normal lives, they became aware that during their journey, they had achieved something truly remarkable. They had been successful in preventing those who would abuse the island's true power from wreaking havoc on the world, and they had brought about change in the world.

But they were also aware that their victory was tinged with disappointment. Along the way, they had lost friends and allies, and they were aware that the sacrifices that those people had made would never be forgotten.

They lamented their losses, but at the same time, they were aware that they needed to move on with their lives. They were obligated to keep the island's secrets safe and to ensure that its real power was never abused in the future.

As a result, they put in countless hours of labor, drawing on their experience and expertise to make the world a better place. They went all over the world, offering assistance to people who were in need and spreading the word about the island's real power.

However, they were also aware that there were still people who would try to abuse the real power that the island possessed. As a result, they made preparations for the worst-case scenario, as they were aware that they might have to engage in another conflict in the future.

After that, the day finally came. Someone or some people had found the location of the Forbidden Island, and they were making preparations to conquer it.

The travelers were aware that time was of the essence and needed to move quickly. Knowing that the future of the world was once again at stake, they gathered their allies and prepared for the imminent invasion.

They fought valiantly, employing all of their abilities and the wealth of knowledge they possessed, to preserve the island and its mysteries. And after what seemed like hours of bloody struggle, the invaders were ultimately victorious.

However, the victory had a sour aftertaste. They had suffered another setback along the way, losing both friends and allies, and they were well aware that the battle was far from over.

They continued their journey in this manner, maintaining a state of constant vigilance and readiness for the worst possible outcome. They were aware that their journey would never really be over as long as there were people who wanted to abuse the island's genuine power. This was something they had come to terms with.

However, they were also aware that the world had changed as a result of their actions. They had saved the world from those who would abuse the real power of the island, and they had improved the lives of a countless number of individuals through their efforts.

The travelers knew that their journey was not over even as they sailed away from the island where they had been forbidden to set foot. They were also filled with a sense of hope and determination, knowing that they had the strength and the knowledge to face whatever challenges lay ahead of them, and this gave them a sense of confidence that they would prevail.

Chapter 30: Return to the Forbidden Island

As the travelers proceeded on their journey, they were unable to shake the feeling that their job was not yet finished, despite their best efforts. They were aware that they had been successful in keeping the island's secrets safe and in harnessing its true power for the greater good, but they were also aware that there was much more work to be done.

As a result, they came to the conclusion that it would be best to go back to the Forbidden Island. They were well aware that the island concealed a great deal of information, and they were intent on finding out what it was.

They noticed that the island had changed as they got closer to it while they were sailing there. They had never witnessed anything like the new structures, new people, and new technologies that they discovered.

They made it to the shore, where they were met by a group of people who had been standing by in anticipation of their arrival. They were astounded to see the travelers because they knew the role that those individuals had played in the development of the island.

The group of people explained that they had been working to uncover the mysteries surrounding the island by making use of the information and the expertise that the previous visitors had left behind.

After that, they were let in on the biggest secret the island had to offer. There was a secret temple buried very deeply below the surface of the island, and it was said to be the source of the island's true power.

They couldn't believe what they had just seen. Ancient artifacts and potent magic were housed inside the temple, both of which had the potential to make the world a better place if only they were used.

They were aware, however, that if the power of the temple was abused, it could lead to disastrous consequences. As a result, they collaborated with the other individuals to make sure that the power emanating from the temple was put to beneficial use.

They embarked on a journey around the world, using the power of the temple to assist those in need and to effect positive change on a global scale. They were conscious of the fact that they had succeeded in achieving something truly remarkable.

The travelers knew that their journey was not over even as they sailed away from the island where they had been forbidden to set foot. They were obligated to keep the island's mysteries safe and to watch out for anyone who might try to abuse the island's real potential.

However, they were also aware that the world had changed as a result of their actions. They had saved the world from those who would abuse the real power of the island, and they had improved the lives of a countless number of individuals through their efforts.

And they were well aware that their travels would not end as long as there were those who sought to abuse the real power that the island possessed. They were also filled with a sense of hope and determination, knowing that they had the strength and the knowledge to face whatever challenges lay ahead of them, and this gave them a sense of confidence that they would prevail.

Also by Eliza Grey

The School for Gifted Teens: A Young Adult Fantasy
The Secret Society of the Night: A Young Adult Mystery
The Forbidden Island: A Race Against Time

About the Publisher

Accepting manuscripts in the most categories. We love to help people get their words available to the world.

Revival Waves of Glory focus is to provide more options to be published. We do traditional paperbacks, hardcovers, audio books and ebooks all over the world. A traditional royalty-based publisher that offers self-publishing options, Revival Waves provides a very author friendly and transparent publishing process, with President Bill Vincent involved in the full process of your book. Send us your manuscript and we will contact you as soon as possible.

Contact: Bill Vincent at rwgpublishing@yahoo.com

www.ingramcontent.com/pod-product-compliance
Lightning Source LLC
LaVergne TN
LVHW041650060526
838200LV00040B/1782